Every new generation of children is enthralled by the famous stories in our Well-loved Tales series. Younger ones love to have the story read to them. Older children will enjoy the exciting stories in an easy-to-read text.

Published by Ladybird Books Ltd Loughborough Leicestershire UK
Ladybird Books Inc Lewiston Maine 04240 USA

The Big Pancake

retold for easy reading
by VERA SOUTHGATE M A B Com

illustrated by
GILLIAN HURRY

Ladybird Books

Once upon a time, there was a mother who had seven little boys — seven, hungry, little boys.

One day, the mother began to
make a very big pancake for her
seven, hungry, little boys.

She took flour, salt, eggs and
milk, and mixed a batter.

Then she melted some butter in
her biggest frying-pan.

Then the mother poured the
batter into the big frying-pan.

It made a very big pancake –
a huge pancake – to feed seven,
hungry, little boys.

The seven little boys watched the pancake as it cooked.

"We are hungry," they said. "Is the pancake ready yet?"

Their mother lifted up one side
of the pancake and looked
underneath.

"It is just turning golden,"
she said.

"Is it ready to eat?" asked the
seven little boys.

"Oh, no!" said their mother. "I must toss it yet. I must toss it up in the air, to turn it over, so that the other side will turn golden. Then it will be ready!"

"Oh dear!" thought the pancake. "I must not wait until my other side is golden or I shall be all eaten up by seven, hungry, little boys. And that will be the end of me!

"I will run away," thought the pancake. "Yes, I will run right away from seven, hungry, little boys."

The mother took the frying-pan
in both hands and tossed the
pancake high in the air.

Then she held out the frying-pan
ready to catch the pancake as it
turned in the air.

"Oh, no, you don't!" said the pancake to itself.

It gave a flip in the air, missed the frying-pan and landed on the floor.

Then, with one side golden and the other side pale, it rolled away on its edge, like a very big penny.

The pancake rolled out of the door and away down the road.

"Stop!" shouted the mother, with her frying-pan still in her hand.

"Stop!" she shouted, as she ran after the pancake.

Faster and faster rolled the pancake, away down the road.

The seven, hungry, little boys
ran down the road behind their
mother.

"Stop!" they shouted. "We
want to eat you!"

"Oh, no!" said the pancake as it rolled on, faster and faster. "I don't want to be eaten by seven, hungry, little boys."

Soon the pancake passed a man.

"Stop!" shouted the man. "You look like a delicious pancake. Please let me eat you."

"Oh, no!" said the pancake. "I don't want to be eaten. A mother couldn't catch me. Seven little boys couldn't catch me. And I won't let *you* catch me!"

Then the pancake rolled on,
faster and faster.

The man joined in behind the
seven, hungry, little boys and the
mother. And they all ran after the
big pancake.

Soon the pancake passed a cat.

"Stop!" shouted the cat. "You look like a delicious pancake. Please let me eat you."

"Oh, no!" said the pancake. "I don't want to be eaten. A mother couldn't catch me. Seven little boys couldn't catch me. A man couldn't catch me. And I won't let *you* catch me!"

29

Then the pancake rolled on,
faster and faster.

The cat joined in behind the
man and the seven, hungry,
little boys and the mother.
And they all ran after
the big pancake.

Soon the pancake passed a cock.

"Stop!" shouted the cock. "You look like a delicious pancake. Please let me eat you."

"Oh, no!" said the pancake. "I don't want to be eaten. A mother couldn't catch me. Seven little boys couldn't catch me. A man couldn't catch me. A cat couldn't catch me. And I won't let *you* catch me!"

Then the pancake rolled on,
faster and faster.

The cock joined in behind the
cat and the man and the seven,
hungry, little boys and the mother.
And they all ran after the big
pancake.

Soon the pancake passed a duck.

"Stop!" shouted the duck.

"You look like a delicious
pancake. Please let me eat you."

"Oh, no!" said the pancake. "I don't want to be eaten. A mother couldn't catch me. Seven little boys couldn't catch me. A man couldn't catch me. A cat couldn't catch me. A cock couldn't catch me. And I won't let *you* catch me!"

Then the pancake rolled on, faster and faster.

The duck joined in behind the cock and the cat and the man and the seven, hungry, little boys and the mother. And they all ran after the big pancake.

Soon the pancake passed a cow.

"Stop!" shouted the cow. "You look like a delicious pancake. Please let me eat you."

"Oh, no!" said the pancake. "I don't want to be eaten. A mother couldn't catch me. Seven little boys couldn't catch me. A man couldn't catch me. A cat couldn't catch me. A cock couldn't catch me. A duck couldn't catch me. And I won't let *you* catch me!"

Then the pancake rolled on,
faster and faster.

The cow joined in behind the
duck and the cock and the cat and
the man and the seven, hungry,
little boys and the mother. And
they all ran after the big pancake.

Soon the pancake passed a pig.

"Where are you going in such a hurry?" asked the pig.

"I am running away from a
mother, seven, hungry, little boys,
a man, a cat, a cock, a duck, and a
cow," said the big pancake. "They
all want to eat me, and I don't
want to be eaten up."

"Of course you don't want to be eaten up!" said the pig, as he ran along beside the pancake. "I never heard of such a thing!"

Soon the pancake and the pig
came to a river.

"Now, what am I going to do?"
the pancake asked the pig. "I can't
swim!"

"But I can swim!" said the pig.
"You get onto my snout and I'll
take you across the river."

So the pancake rolled onto the
pig's snout.

Then the pig opened his mouth
and gobbled up the pancake.

And it *was* a delicious pancake!

That was the end of the big pancake.

So the mother and the seven, hungry, little boys and the man and the cat and the cock and the duck and the cow never *did* catch the big pancake!